BILL AND THE Google-Eyed GOBLINS

By
Alice Schertle

Illustrated by
Patricia Coombs

For Katie, who named the goblins

 Inquiries should be addressed to Lothrop, Lee & Shepard Books, a division of William Morrow & Company, Inc., 105 Madison Avenue, New York, New York 10016.
Printed in Hong Kong.

First Edition 1 2 3 4 5 6 7 8 9 10

Library of Congress Cataloging in Publication Data Schertle, Alice. Bill and the google-eyed goblins. Summary: A young man who loves to dance is captured by the goblins beneath the hill and must challenge them to a dance contest in order to escape. [1. Fairy tales. 2. Dancing—Fiction] I. Coombs, Patricia, ill. II. Title. PZ8.S2775Bi 1987 [E] 86-7420
ISBN 0-688-06701-8 ISBN 0-688-06702-6 (lib. bdg.)

Young Bill was a born dancer. He could hear music in the whistle of a wintry wind or the rattle of dry leaves or the bawling of a newborn calf. And music set Bill's fingers snapping and his toes a-tapping.

The neighbors often saw Bill jigging away, twirling and spinning to a tune only he could hear. "There's that dancing fool," they'd say, and they'd shake their heads. "That boy will never amount to anything."

Still, as good neighbors will, they tried to change Bill for the better.

"Plant a seed, boy!" said the farmer. "Prune a tree! Think fields and furrows, horse and plow!"

Bill gave it a try, and he would have done right well if he hadn't heard music in the *clop! clop! clop!* of the horse's hooves and the soft *chunk! chunk!* of the plow. While Bill danced a jig over the newly turned earth, the horse dragged the plow into the pond.

"Dancing won't put a loaf on the table," warned the baker. "Think pies, boy! Think sugar and eggs and a pinch of salt!"

Bill went to work for the baker, and he would have done fine if the pots and pans hadn't made such lovely music. *Clatter! Clash! Clang!* Bill set the pie tins in a row. *Glop! Glop! Glop!* He beat the batter in the bowl. *Chooka! Chooka! Chooka!* He shook out the salt. He kept time to the music with his feet, and pretty soon he was spinning around the kitchen. The pies might turn from brown to black, but there was dancing to be done.

The neighbors shook their heads. "A dancing fool," they said. "He'll never amount to anything."

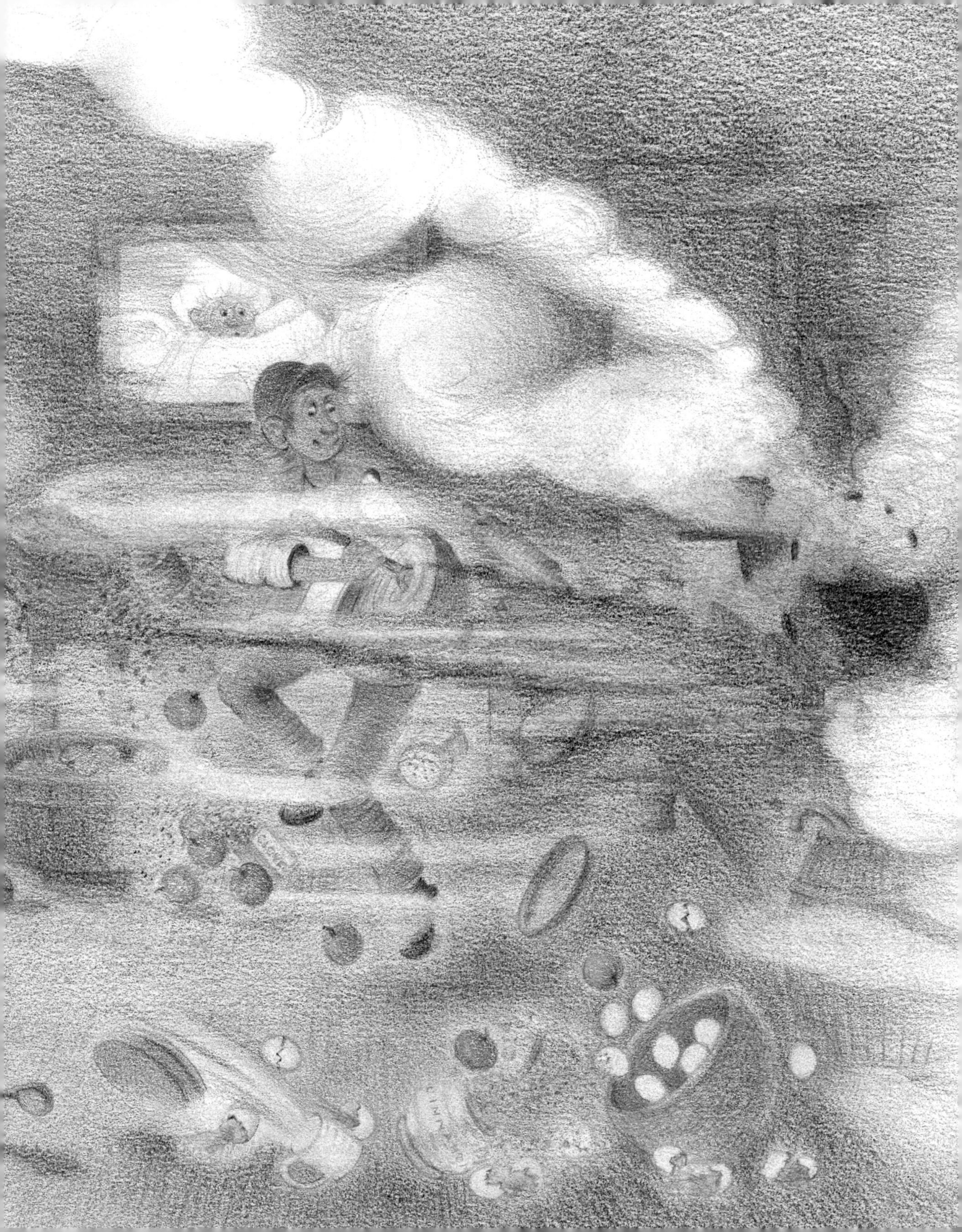

One night, the eve of All Hallows, Bill was wakened from a sound sleep by music more beautiful than any he had ever heard before. Sweeter than water over stones, that music was, and it set Bill's heart pounding. In an instant he was out of bed, through the door, and dancing up the road. A full moon, big and round as a mill wheel, rolled through the sky, and the stars themselves spun round to the music.

Bill followed the sound to the top of a hill crowned by a circle of velvety moss.

Now, Bill was nobody's fool, in spite of what the neighbors thought. He wasn't one to go stepping into fairy rings. But the music had him, and his two feet just danced him right into the center of the circle.

With a great cracking sound, the hill split apart like a ripe melon. A dozen little google-eyed goblins grabbed Bill by the legs and dragged him down.

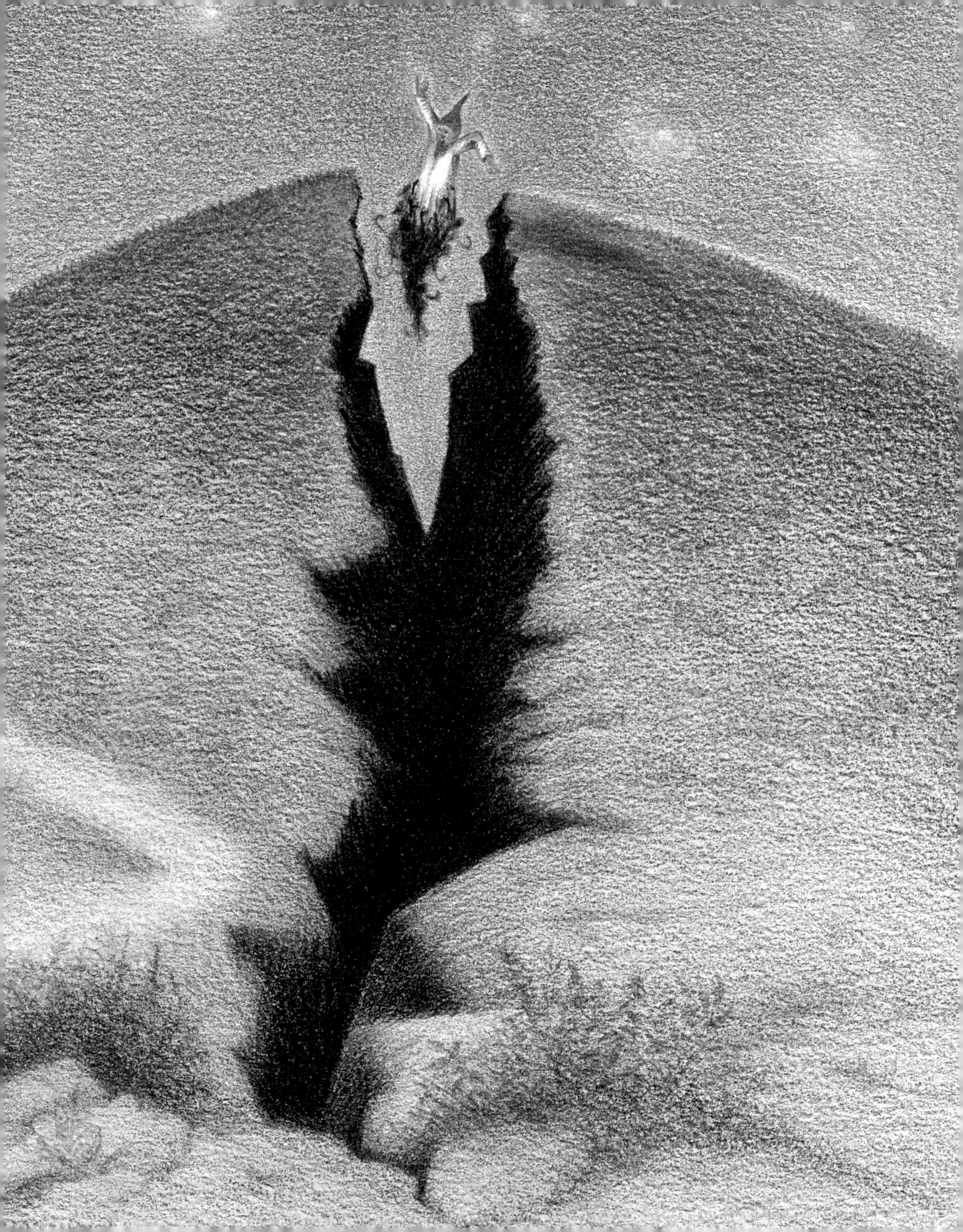

Bill was hustled along a dim corridor and into a great hall aglow with jack-o'-lanterns and aswarm with grinning goblins. On a toadstool throne sat the goblin king, gnawing on a bone.

The king held up his hand, the music stopped, and the great hall became quiet as a tomb. "Welcome, Bill!" he shouted. "I've been expecting you!"

"Thanks a million," said Bill, "but I'm afraid I can't stay."

"Not so fast." The goblin king took Bill by the hand and led him to the center of the hall, where gold coins were piled as high as the ceiling. "Before you leave, you'll oblige me by polishing these," the king told him. "Make a good job of it, Bill. I like to see my face in 'em."

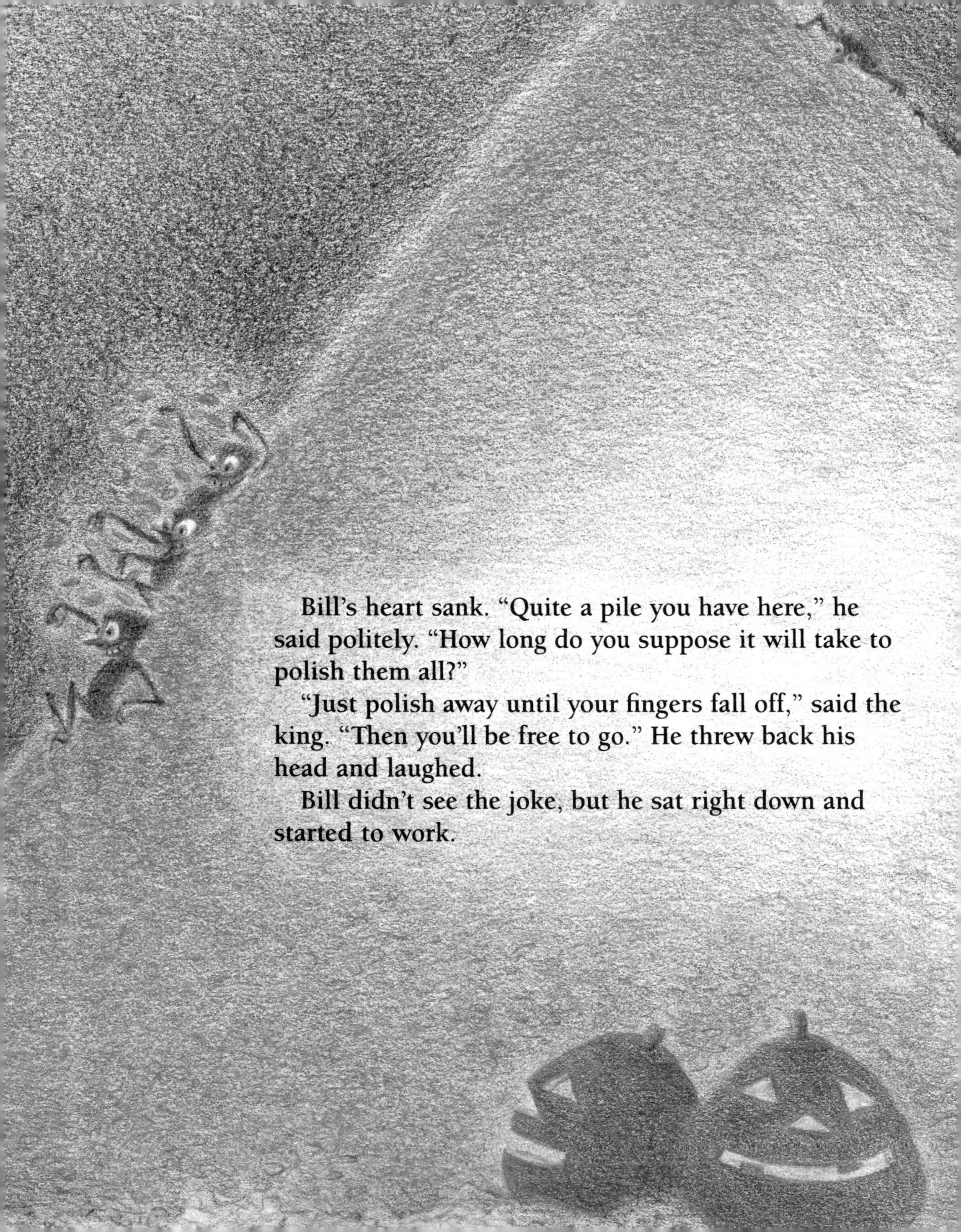

Bill's heart sank. "Quite a pile you have here," he said politely. "How long do you suppose it will take to polish them all?"

"Just polish away until your fingers fall off," said the king. "Then you'll be free to go." He threw back his head and laughed.

Bill didn't see the joke, but he sat right down and started to work.

Pretty soon the music struck up again, and the goblins began to dance gleefully in a tight little circle around Bill. Keeping one eye on the goblins, Bill polished and rubbed for all he was worth. After a while he shouted, "That's the worst excuse for dancing I ever saw!"

Well, that stopped the goblins in midstep. They gathered around Bill, shaking their fists at him. "I suppose you think you can do better!" screamed the goblin king.

"I can," said Bill. "I'm a born dancer."

"We'll just see about that!" the king cried.

The next thing Bill knew, three goblins had dragged him to his feet. He tried not to see the wicked little faces glaring at him from every side. Instead, he imagined himself dancing across a green meadow with the sun warm on his back and a fresh breeze blowing. And Bill danced as he had never danced before.

Pretty soon the goblins were clapping their hands and tapping their feet and nodding their heads to the music.

Bill folded his arms tightly across his chest. "No hands!" he shouted. "Can a goblin do that?"

In no time at all the goblins were leaping and spinning, their hairy arms clutching their chests.

Bill caught up his left foot in his hand. "One foot!" he shouted. "How about that?"

And then the whole ghoulish throng, with Bill in the middle, were hopping out one-footed rhythms on the floor.

So Bill flipped into a handstand, shouting, "No feet at all, then! How about that?" Soon the hall was full of goblins dancing on their hands.

Finally Bill shouted, "Anyone can dance with both eyes open!" He pulled his nightcap down over his face. "No eyes, goblins! No eyes!"

Every goblin snatched up a sash or a scarf. The hall trembled with sightless dancers turning and tumbling, leaping and lunging.

As the music rose to a feverish pitch, Bill slid the nightcap from his head and made his way to the pile of gold. He filled the cap with coins. Then he was off down the dark corridor, running as if the google-eyed goblins were hot on his heels.

And soon they were. The corridor echoed with howls of rage and shook with the thunder of pursuing feet. Bill could almost feel the goblins' reaching fingers on the back of his neck.

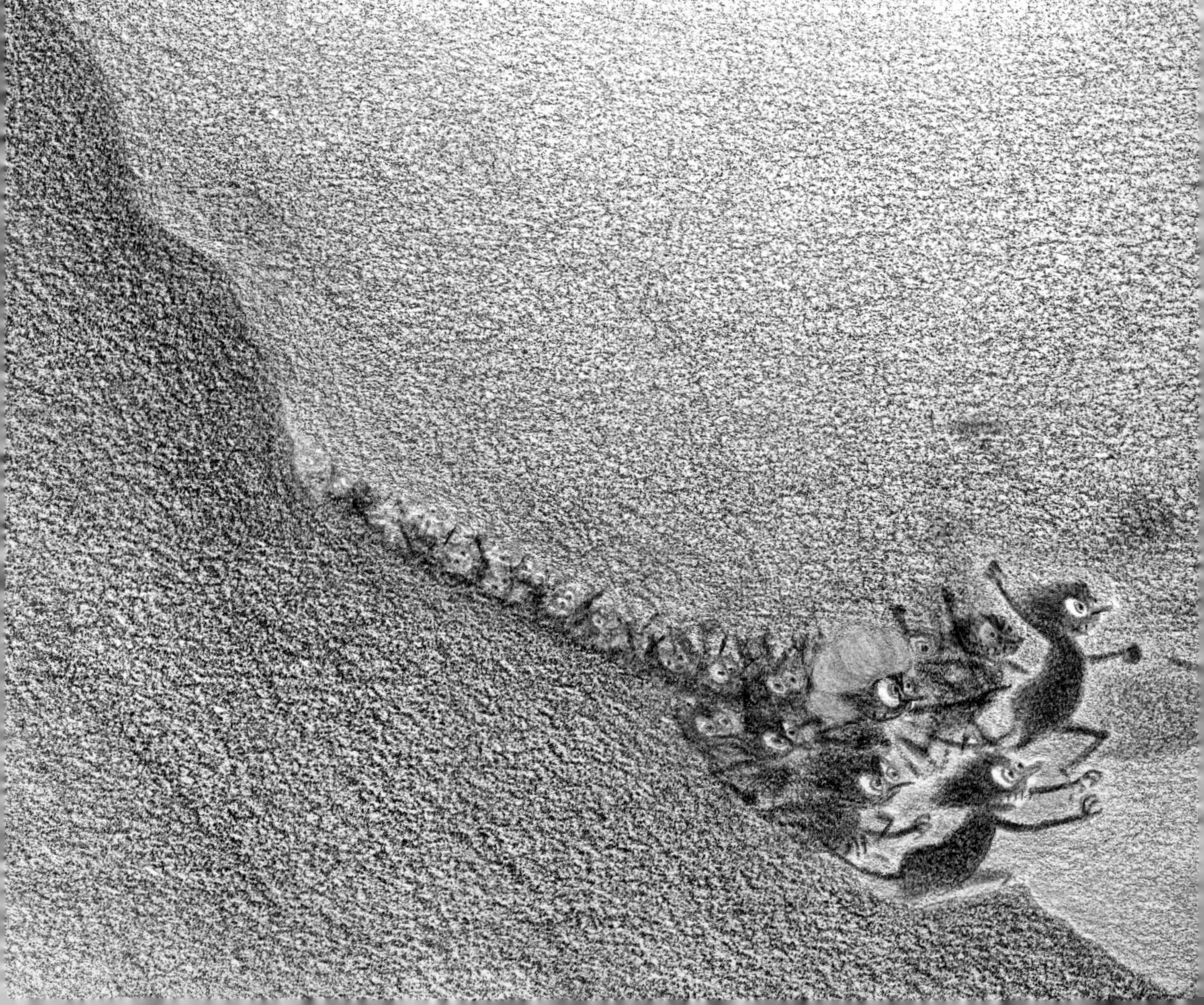

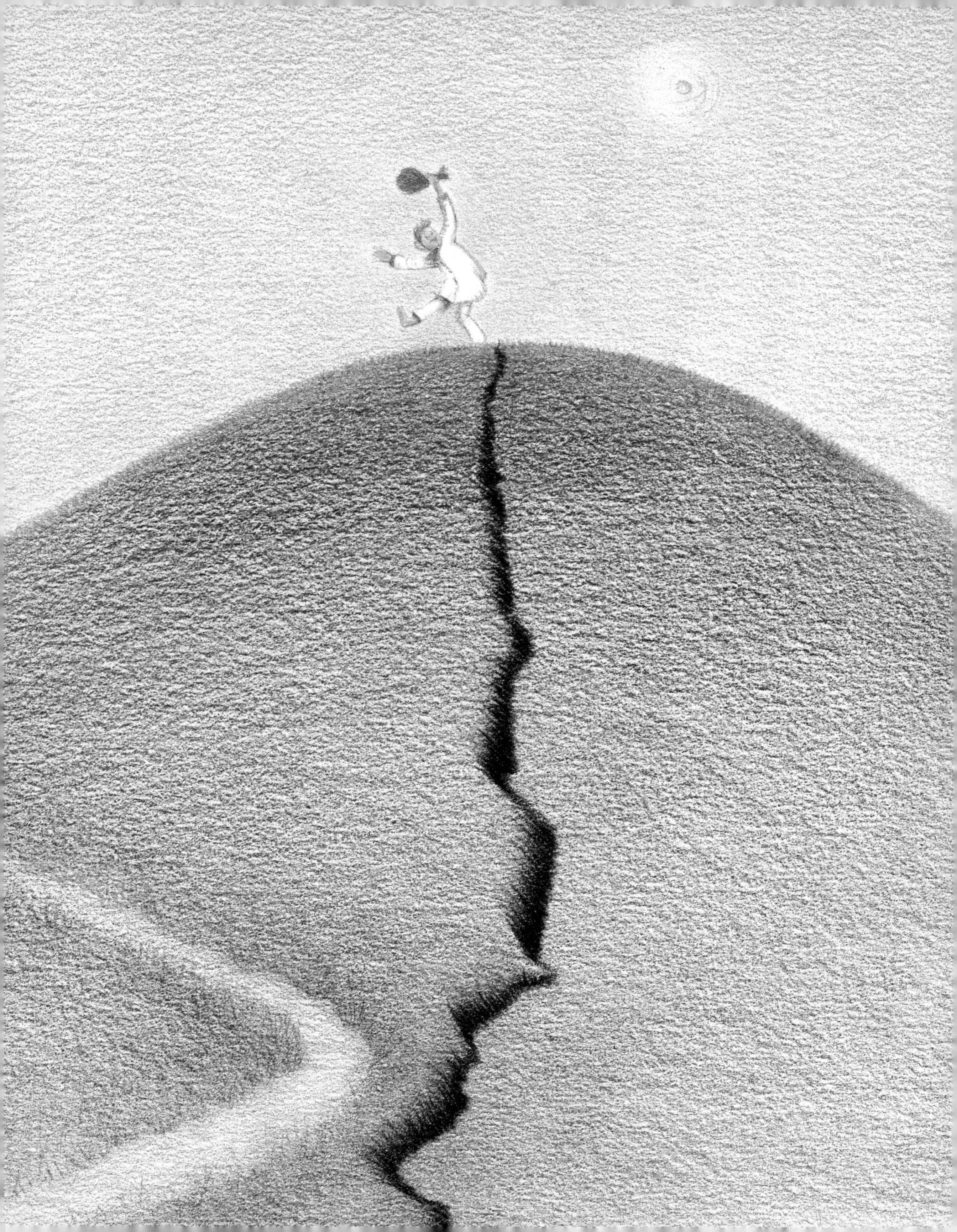

Up ahead, he saw the glimmer of a faint star through the crack in the hill. But the two sides of the opening were coming together with a dull rumbling. Bill kept his eyes on that fading star, and with the last strength in his body made a mighty leap. He grabbed the edge and pulled himself out into the fresh air of a dawning day. As the first rays of the morning sun touched the top of the hill, the great crack slammed shut behind him.

With the goblin gold, Bill built himself a fine big house. He bought a new suit of clothes and shiny shoes with brass buckles. The neighbors took to tipping their hats when they met him on the road. And when they saw him dancing across a meadow to a tune only he could hear, they'd smile and nod their heads.

"Bill's a born dancer," one would say to the other. "I always knew the lad would do well."

Bill himself often thought of the great hall beneath the hill and the google-eyed goblins with their hoard of gold. But if the goblin music ever again leaked in through the bedroom window, Bill never knew, for he always went to sleep with cotton in his ears.